The Spy in the Alps

The Royal Crown: Part 1

Frances Rose

*To my love, Morgan, who believes in me when
I don't believe in myself, and to my family,
who support me unconditionally.*

Contents

Title Page
Dedication
Chapter 1   1
Chapter 2   9
Chapter 3   27
Chapter 4   33
Chapter 5   52
Chapter 6   65

Chapter 1

Diego Salvador stood between rail cars, his strong legs bestrode the gap separating them. In front of him lay the end of the road. He had tracked the thief to this storage compartment. He pulled out his pistol, and readied himself to take the thief down, with force if necessary. With his breath held, he put his hand on the door knob and with great strength threw the door open. The compartment was dark, and he could only hear the rushing air outside the train car as the locomotive charged towards its destination in the Alps. He held his weapon in front of him, "You may as well come out. I know I have you trapped. It wasn't a very smart move coming here to check on your stolen goods."

"It's a good thing you're pretty," came a buzzing electronic voice from somewhere to his left.

Diego's hands gripped his pistol tighter, scanning the darkness to no avail.

The modulated voice spoke again, "I would never stash the goods in here. I just needed to know what you looked like." Suddenly, like a flash a gloved hand came flying from the darkness twisting his pistol out of his hands. He heard a clanging sound behind him, and spun to see his pistol slide out the open door and over the edge of the train, lost. "Now that I know who's trying to follow me, I can absolve you of the responsibility. Hold on tight." Diego fell flat on his back as the train suddenly lurched to a grinding halt. He gasped for breath as the wind was knocked out of him. He saw a flash of white as a hooded masked figure sprinted past him and out of the train car. Diego knew he had no time to lose and struggled to get to his feet even as breathing eluded him. Staggering up and towards the door of the compartment, the figure was already gone. Cursing to himself, he crossed the gap between the cars, and opened the door, knowing that his quarry might be lost. Refusing to admit defeat, he ran as fast as his legs would carry him. He wouldn't lose the thief.

Desirée sighed contentedly as she looked out the train window at the picturesque Alps passing by. She had always wanted to visit France, and so far it had been an absolute dream, minus an unexpected layover in Athens on the way there. She had always wanted to go, and had a wonderful start to her trip in Paris, the City of Lights, and it was as beautiful and romantic as she had always hoped. The food, the sidewalk cafes, the art, the men with their accents and hot lips, it had been everything she could have hoped for... though she had needed to slap a man one evening at a bar for getting a little too familiar. All in all though, a perfect start to her trip.

Desirée thumbed through her trip itinerary, and what an itinerary it was. She checked Paris off the top of the list, and looked at some of the other highlights: Rome, Athens, Cairo... this was a long vacation, but a long time coming, and she deserved it. Satisfied, she leaned back in her seat, looking forward to the next destination, a ski resort in Morzine, France.

Glancing out the window, she caught a reflection of her wavy, brown hair that cascaded past her shoulders. Her major selling point, an agent had once told her early in her acting career. She had taken it to heart, as the agent had then proceeded to tell her that she, "hadn't much else going for her."

'What an asshole,' she thought to herself. She had more than made up for that early sting by being the best stage actress this side of the millennium, and she had been told that agent no longer worked in New York.

Desirée was startled out of her thoughts as the train jolted violently and came to a stop, spilling her out of her seat. She struggled to stand upright, as she heard a compartment door next to hers slam shut. After a few moments of collecting herself, she open her compartment's door and stood astonished as she saw a stormy, dark-complexioned man at the end of the train's corridor sprinting down towards her.

"What's going on?" called out Desirée to the man as he hurtled towards her like destiny itself.

"I am sorry, señorita, there's no time to explain," he exclaimed as he shot past her.

Desirée was more than slightly shocked at the man, and turned to look at the figure that had passed by as he entered the next car. 'Maybe I can find out for myself,' she decided.

She began following him towards the next car when a door to her side opened, and a younger, blonde woman stepped out of the compartment in front of her blocking her way.

"C'est inacceptable!" the woman cried in French. Furiously, the woman spun on a heel towards Desirée, looked her up and down, and in a heavy accent drawled, "You are American, no?"

Desirée was floored by the disdain that had been tossed at her, "Yes, and you're a bitch, no?"

The blonde woman looked taken aback for a moment, before bursting into laughter, "I like you! You remind me of my mother. What is your name, madame?"

"Desirée, et vous?" Desirée replied using her French. This woman may like her, but she didn't like this blonde bimbo.

"I am called Charlotte," came the reply, with a knowing smirk. Charlotte extended a gloved hand outwards gesturing to her compartment, "Would you like to come in? I have been very bored and would welcome the company. The train, he is taking longer than expected to arrive."

Desirée weighed the options in her head, and decided that the young, blonde Charlotte might at least help make the time go faster, "I'd be delighted."

"C'est magnifique!"

"Just give me one moment to grab some of my things from my compartment, and I shall join you."

"As you wish."

And with that, Charlotte sashayed back to her room, and left Desirée to grab her things. Not too long after, Desirée found herself sitting with Charlotte, listening to Charlotte chatter effervescently on about her recent trips around Europe, including her most recent trip to Spain.

"It is quite ridiculous, this siesta that they have. They treat it like the British treat their tea! It happens at the absolute worst time of day, too! How else am I supposed to go shopping and find clothes to go dancing in! I will say that the dancing is...." she smiled to herself, "...well it makes their siesta worth it. Tell me Desirée, for someone with a name that means Desired, you seem like your days of man hunting are at an end."

Desirée bristled, "I manage fine."

Charlotte laughed, "Perhaps, but still, I can only imagine, someone of your advancing years must have some good stories to tell.

Desirée forced a smile, "A lady doesn't kiss and tell."

At this Charlotte fell into a fit of laughter, wiping her eyes, "I suppose that makes me unladylike, but I don't care. I pride myself on having enjoyed my travels, and the men I have met. I have a theory that the way the men are in a country tells you all that you must know about that country. For example, I visited the United States when I was in university, and I found the men there far too direct and expectant. A woman wants to be won, no? There was no flair, no profound words of adoration, nothing to set the heart racing!"

Desirée decided to keep her exasperation to herself and played along, "Which men would you say are the best then?"

"But of course, this is a difficult question, yet each country has its own charms. The men in France, they excel in the art of conversation; the men in Italy, they are passionate and declare that they would die should you not love them; the men in Greece, they are dark and strong.."

"And the men of Spain?"

"I was getting to that! The Spanish are passionate and sensual much like the Italians, but they are less dramatic, they are more ready to woo you with a dance or a song than with declarations of endless devotion that expire much too soon. But, nonetheless…"

Desirée tuned out Charlotte as she had grown tired of the conversation, to avoid being rude, she continued to engage with slight murmurs of astonishment or interest. This seemed to suit Charlotte just fine as she continued to speak unabated. Desirée found her mind wandering back to the dark stranger who had passed by earlier. He had been in such a hurry, and why? She decided that there was no use in wondering as she probably would never see him again.

Diego cursed to himself, he had lost the trail of the jewel thief. As a member of the Royal Spanish Service, it was his job to protect the Spanish Royal Family, and that extended to the Crown Jewels, too. He had tracked the thief from Madrid to Paris, and he was certain that the thief was on this train, and had finally had the masked bandit cornered in the final car of the train when the criminal pulled the emergency brake. He had lost the trail, no matter how fast he pursued the outlaw. He walked back to his compartment and tried running over what he knew about the thief. Unfortunately, there was little to go off of. Somehow, the person had managed to avoid world class security systems, yet had left a trail leading to Paris, and, he believed, to this train. This was shaping up to be the most difficult case of his career, and he couldn't afford to lose. Not again.

Diego got back to his room on the train as he felt the locomotive gathering speed again. "Any luck?" he heard from inside. Diego walked in to see his older French handler who had been assigned to him by DGSE and Interpol to make sure he followed the laws of France while operating there. Diego took in the grayed temples and lines that contoured Jacques du Lac's face. It was a face weathered out of stone.

"No, Monsieur du Lac. I'm sure you felt my failure from here."

"I did."

"And?"

"And what, Diego? I am not concerned with you losing this thief, this Le Renard."

"I find that a callous remark."

"You misunderstand me, Diego. I'm simply stating that this train has but one destination, and only one. Even though the thief may know you are behind them, whoever it is cannot leave too soon after arriving, for fear of arousing suspicion. Do not worry, you will have some time to discover your quarry."

With that, Jacques took out his newspaper and began to read. Diego had to admit to himself that Jacques had a point. Yet, frustrated, he also felt that the older man couldn't understand. He knew that the old man didn't have to hear the roar or feel the heat on his skin every night like he did. When he closed his eyes, he could still see her face...

'No.' Diego thought furiously to himself. He couldn't let himself be stuck in the past. He couldn't. He couldn't. Weary and still trying to get his breath completely back, Diego sat opposite of Jacques and attempted to get some sleep. There were a few hours before they would arrive, and he needed to be rested. He had to win this time.

Chapter 2

Finally, they had arrived. The rest of the train ride had been less than pleasant, doubly so when Charlotte had touched on an old nerve asking about Desirée's family. Desirée didn't like having to tell people about her family, nor about her mother. Thankfully, Charlotte had been understanding of this and dropped that point of conversation immediately. In fact, she had even then invited Desirée to her family's ski lodge, to which Desirée politely, if insincerely, responded that she would have to consider the offer.

Desirée stepped off of the train onto the wintry platform in Morzine. The midwinter air had a delicious bite, and Desirée was excited to explore every nook and cranny of this little resort town. From the platform she could see the warm lights from the buildings reflecting off the snow, creating a cozy haze over the valley of Aulps.

"I absolutely adore this town," came Charlotte's voice behind her, "Come let us go!"

Desirée grimaced and followed the bouncing blonde hair in front of her, she had made the unfortunate discovery that Charlotte was staying at the same hotel as she was. She supposed it might be helpful, at least, since she felt her French was only just passable, and Charlotte seemed to know where she was going.

As if reading Desirée's mind, Charlotte called over her shoulder, "Do not worry your pretty little head if you should get lost, this town she caters to many British people, almost everyone speaks English." Charlotte's condescension, all the more grating for how much younger Charlotte was, notwithstanding, the evening seemed full of promise. Desirée gripped her bags as she exited the train station onto the snow-strewn street of the township. The road was bustling with late afternoon traffic and opposite her she saw a sidewalk overflowing with brightly dressed men and women trafficking boutiques containing the latest winter fashion straight from Milan. People were clutching bags from their shopping, shining in iridescent reds, yellows, and blues that popped against the white of the snow along the way. She heard music off to her left towards a main thoroughfare, and the smell of cinnamon roasted nuts hung in the air like perfume. The sound of voices rang in the streets, often punctuated by laughter. All around her was excitement, energy, and beauty. In the distance and surrounding her she could see the Alps, down lower in the valley she was able to spot a gorgeous lake, and there were light flurries in the air. It was perfect.

Desirée kept following Charlotte street after street and finally came to her hotel, near the center of the town. The hotel was old fashioned and beautiful, yet fairly modern, in an almost anachronistic way. Through the double doors of the hotel, they entered a luxurious lobby, ornamented in gold, with rich leather and mahogany furniture round the room, all framing a large fireplace on one wall. As they walked up to the front desk, Charlotte, thankfully, insisted on getting her room first, which happily would allow Desirée to say her good bye without seeming rude. Charlotte walked up to the front desk, leaving Desirée alone for the first time in hours. Desirée gazed out the windows of the lobby, it had begun to lightly snow, and the world for everything seemed like a miracle. She had never imagined that so beautiful a place could actually exist. She watched as people walked around, locals and tourists alike. Going about their various businesses. She wondered if living in Morzine year round would cause the magic she felt to fade, or if it would be like living in a storybook your entire life. She was caught off guard when she noticed the Spanish man from the train standing with two older men. One of them seemed to know him, and they were both talking to the third. The third man lifted a hand and pointed at the hotel where she was staying. They appeared to thank him, and started walking across the street towards the building. She watched the Spanish man intently. He was walking towards the building like a tiger stalking, readying to pounce.

Charlotte's voice broke her focus, "Please don't forget my invitation, my dear!"

Desirée spun, and flashed a fake smile, "Don't worry, I wont!"

With that Charlotte nodded, smiling back, and bounded towards the elevator. With Charlotte gone, the front desk was empty and Desirée grabbed her bags and went to it. The man behind the front desk was easily 30 years Desirée's senior, somewhere in his 70s, but he seemed kind enough.

"How may I help you?" he inquired in a shockingly proper British accent.

"Checking in under the name of Woods. Desirée Woods?"

"But of course, mademoiselle, it shall only be a moment." His eyes flicked over the books behind the desk. "Yes, here we are. Suite 508. Our very best, if I do say so myself!" he laughed.

"I'm sure you say that to everyone," quipped back Desirée playfully. She liked this man. He reminded her of her grandfather. She winced. When she was thinking of family, thoughts of her mother often came unbidden. She did her best to shake it off.

"Yes, I do," he smiled gently seemingly ignoring her look of pain. "But, it is a very fine room!" He handed over the room key, and called over the bellhop. "This is my grandson Vincent, he will help you, and if there's anything you need please don't hesitate to ask."

"Thank you very much, Monsieur..."

"Vincent, mademoiselle."

"Ah, your grandson is named after you?"

"In a way, he is named after his father, who was named after me, as I was after my father, and he after his."

"That's interesting, which Vincent are you?"

"The 19th Miss Woods. Is there anything else you need?" he smiled politely but clearly wished to end the conversation.

"No, thank you very much," she replied, and with that Vincent the 21st took her bags and led her to the elevator. Desirée heard the front doors to the lobby open, and a blast of chilly air caressed the back of her head. She turned and looked over her shoulder and saw the Spaniard with the older man, dusting off the snow from their jackets as they walked up to Vincent the 19th.

ding

Desirée looked back, and the elevator had arrived for her. She got on to it being gestured forward by the younger Vincent, but not before taking one last look at the lobby. The older man was talking to Vincent the 19th, and the Spaniard was looking around. The elevators doors started closing, and suddenly his eyes snapped to her, making contact with hers. In his eyes, she saw intensity, hunger, and desire. Then he was gone, and the elevator lifted her to the fifth floor. The doors opened with another *ding* and Vincent the 19th led her to her room.

"Here you are mademoiselle, if there is anything else you need please do not hesitate to ask!" She thanked him for his help, and he left her standing in front of the door with her luggage. Desirée stood for a moment trying to forget the Spanish man's eyes. They had been a deep dark brown, nearly black, and she felt like they had seen through to her core. She shook her head, Spaniards were nice, and he was an attractive man from what she had seen, but she had more pressing matters to attend to. She always loved opening a hotel room for the first time, it was like opening a Christmas present. She took out her key and opened the door to the darkened room. She pulled her luggage in behind her, and shut the door. She found a light switch slightly off to her right, and flipped it up.

The room was breathtaking, and she walked further to take in the room around her. it was wonderfully crafted with intricate woodwork on the bedposts and the desk. On the left side, opposite the bed, was a stone fireplace set and simply waiting for a match, and at the end of the room were two gleaming white french doors which opened out onto a private balcony. There was a door to Desirée's right which opened into the bathroom. In addition to the normal accouterments, as she walked in she was greeted by rich marble counters, a deep Jacuzzi tub, and to the right an open air rainfall shower. She let out a contented sigh, and decided to take a hot, relaxing bubble bath.

Desirée set the tub to fill up and undressed quickly. She soon found her tense, travel worn muscles submerged in the tub, the knots slowly unwinding. She sunk deeper and deeper into sublime relaxation. She found the warmth of the tub slowly seeping into her core, warming her after the cold trek from the train station. Looking around, she noticed a remote for a television. She couldn't see anything it could turn on from her vantage point, but on a lark she decided to try to turn on whatever was there. She pressed the power button, and with a click and a sizzle a television turned on in the mirror. She laughed to herself excitedly and started flipping through channels. There was the local weather, followed by one of those singing competitions, a news report about an international thief who had stolen something; channel after channel. Finally, she decided to settle on an interior decorating show, the kind where designers flip a house as a surprise to an overworked mother.

Desirée was engrossed in the new crown molding of a German couple's house when a sharp rapping came from the door to her hotel room. Desirée waited a moment to see if they would go away, but that hope was dashed when the knocking came a second time, even louder than the first. She let out a disappointed breath, yelled, "I'm coming!" and stood out of the bath. She quickly wrapped a towel around herself, and went to the door. Right as she got to the door, the knock came a third, very aggressive time. "I said I was coming!" she exclaimed as she threw open the door angrily.

To her shock, it was the Spanish man again. He seemed similarly shocked at seeing Desirée in her towel, but there was something under that shock as well. Something that made Desirée's pulse race.

"Pardon me," he began, slightly flustered, his face reddening ever so slightly. She noticed that he looked younger than her, but not by much. He had black curly hair, the sort that you would have seen on ancient Greek statue, and with a build to match. He was strong and athletic, but not overly muscle bound like some body builder. His eyes were even darker close up if it was possible, and in those eyes there was the same intensity from before, but something else that she hadn't noticed... sadness? Maybe? She couldn't put her finger on it, but she was transfixed on those eyes when she heard his voice again.

"Miss?"

"Desirée."

"Miss Desirée, I apologise for barging in unannounced like this. My name is Santiago Salazar. I am a journalist, and I was curious if I could interview you for a piece that I'm writing."

Intrigued, Desirée asked, "What sort of piece is this, Mr. Salazar?"

"It's a piece about Morzine, and the travelers that come here."

"That should be fine Mr. Salazar, when would you like to interview me?" Remembering her state, she gestured to herself, "as you can see, I'm not quite in the right state to..."

"How about dinner this evening?" he quickly interjected.

Desirée was slightly taken aback, but not altogether displeased, "That should work fine for me, though I must be clear that this is purely professional, Mr. Salazar."

"Of course! I wouldn't dream of anything else," he agreed.

"Then if that's all?"

"Yes, yes! Shall we say, we meet downstairs in an hour?"

Desirée began to close the door, "That works for me. I will see you then Mr. Salazar."

"Until then!" came the voice from behind the closing door.

Desirée closed the door, and heard the footsteps away from her room. It wasn't until then that she realised how long she had been holding her breath. Santiago was a very attractive man, and there she was just standing in her towel. Her heart was beating out of her chest, and she could feel her blood coursing everywhere through her body. With a start, she jumped from her reverie. She had a date to get ready for! 'No. A meeting,' she thought to herself. She couldn't help but smile remembering the look on his face when he saw her in the towel. She thought of Charlotte's earlier comments about her age and smirked. Maybe she would engage in some man-hunting after all.

Diego turned the corner and called the elevator. His heart was pounding. He hadn't expected to interrupt a woman taking a bath. He could still see her wet towel hugging the curves of her body... he sighed sadly, he knew he couldn't get involved. The whole point of his cover was so that he could get information from people without arousing suspicion. He had studied the itineraries of all the passengers on the train, and had narrowed down the possible suspects to just a few people. One of which had been seen conversing and entering this hotel with the woman he had just interrupted mid-bath. The elevator opened and he stepped inside. Jacques had spoken with the elderly hotel owner at the front desk, and after explaining the situation, Monsieur Vincent had more than happily given them a double room to work out of.

He had to get ready for his meeting with Desirée. Unwanted, images of her kept flooding his mind. She was the most beautiful woman he had ever seen, and he couldn't help but imagine holding her in his arms. The feel of her skin pressed against his, his mouth brushing down her neck... he felt his manhood push against the front of his pants. 'Get a grip,' he thought insistingly. He was here on a mission for the Spanish Crown, and he couldn't let himself get distracted. Distractions lead to mistakes, and mistakes lead to death.

The elevator arrived on his floor, and Diego walked out and proceeded to his room. Opening the door, he heard then saw Jacques snoring loudly on one of the twin beds.

"Jacques. Wake up," he said brusquely. He picked up a pillow from his bed and threw it at the sleeping man. It hit him in the head.

Jacques startled awake, "Putain!" Looking around the room he saw the pillow and then looked at Diego rather unimpressedly, "What is it?"

"While you were snoring, I was setting up a meeting to gather intelligence on one of our suspects, specifically Charlotte Mechant."

Jacques rolled over and sat up on the edge of the bed, "And how did you manage this?"

"I found the woman that she came here with. An American, named Desirée."

"And for this you woke me up?"

"Well, yes."

"Wake me again when you've actually discovered something from your rendezvous." Jacques laid back down and rolled over with his back to Diego. Diego shook his head and went to the bathroom to get ready. He kept reminding himself that he was preparing for intelligence gathering, not a date. This did not stop him from putting on an extra spritz of cologne, however.

Desirée finished her bath and went to her closet where her garment bag was hanging with her all of her dresses. She leafed through them like a catalog and found herself stumped with which dress to pick. She had a short blue one that made her feel taller, but it was too casual. It wasn't that she wanted Santiago to think this was anything other than business, but she also wanted to make sure that she made an impression. Then there was the green dress with a matching blazer. 'No,' she thought, 'TOO business-like.' Every dress she had didn't seem right. She finally pulled out her red cocktail dress. It was her favorite. It made her feel strong and confident, and she'd never met a man yet who could look away when she wore it. 'Plus,' she thought to herself, 'it's one of my classiest dresses, and who knows where we're going to go tonight.' With that, it was decided, the red cocktail dress it was.

Desirée slid into her pantyhose and dress, and turned on the TV while she was putting in her earrings and putting on her makeup. It was another news broadcast about the stolen Spanish jewels. She turned it up out of curiosity, "… and this marks the fifth day since the Crown Jewels of Spain have been stolen. Spanish authorities have identified the thief as none other than Le Renard. This crime marks the latest in a string of thefts attributed to the infamous French cat burglar, including last month's stealing of Picasso's *Composition* from the National Gallery in Athens." She looked up, she had wanted to go there during an unexpected layover in Athens on her way to Paris, but it had been closed, now she knew why. She turned the volume up, "Authorities have not been able to determine the whereabouts of the stolen work, and is asking for anyone with information concerning the theft to come forward." She turned it off. Her meeting with Santiago was soon, and she needed to finish getting ready. She fiddled trying to get her second earring to fasten, thinking that it was deplorable that someone would steal such valuable historical artifacts, though she did have to admit that there was a certain allure to the idea of being a world-infamous burglar. With a snap she felt the clasps fasten. She got up and looked at herself in the mirror, the dress was snug in the right places, her earrings were secured, her heels were perfection, and as soon as she applied a matching red lipstick, she would be ready to meet Santiago. She wondered as she looked for her lipstick if Santiago was even half as excited about this meeting as she was.

Diego fastened his laces. It was nearly time to meet Desirée, and he didn't want to be late. He was about to walk out the door when the phone on the nightstand began to ring. He looked over and saw Jacques had already gotten it.

"Oui, je comprends. Merci beaucoup," came the older man's voice. He hung up the phone. "Well, Diego it seems your search has gotten slightly easier. We've gotten a positive ID from a witness in Athens. Le Renard, is a blonde woman around 170cm tall. And, it seem she had an older brunette accomplice," he continued, "I believe we have more than one suspect who fits." He raised an eyebrow at Diego and smirked, "Bon Appétit."

"Just have the room ready in case I have to bring her back here." He turned on his heel and left without another word. He had to stay focused. He couldn't let himself be distracted by a pair of beautiful eyes. He walked to the elevator. He sincerely hoped that Desirée wasn't involved in this whole mess, but knew that he had to keep an objective eye on the situation. Hoping the Desirée wasn't involved wouldn't magically prevent her from being, and that sort of thing could be dangerous.

Diego found Desirée waiting in the lobby. His eyes almost popped out of his head and his jaw nearly hit the floor. She was wearing a red cocktail dress that hugged every curve, and she was flaunting it proudly. Her hair waterfalled down to her shoulders in brunette curls, and she had on bright red lipstick that drew him in with tender promises. "Desirée," he said from across the room. Desirée turned with the largest eyes he had ever seen, were they always so big?

"Santiago, how are you?" her voice chimed.

"I'm fine, and you?" he said amiably, but cautiously. In spite of himself, he found himself thinking that she certainly couldn't be involved with Le Renard.

"Delightful," she tittered, "Where are we going?"

"I was thinking we could just have dinner at the hotel restaurant here. It's the nicest one in town, and you're dressed perfectly for it."

"Marvelous!" she flashed a smile that melted him.

"After you!" He gestured gallantly. She went ahead of him into the restaurant. He grimaced. This was going to be harder than he thought.

Desirée's heart was a flutter. Santiago was even better looking than earlier, and somehow seemed taller too. Every inch of at least 6'1". He had been the perfect model of a gentleman all evening- he was charming, intelligent, and witty. It may not have been exactly as Charlotte had described Spaniards, but she was happy with the product nonetheless. The wine had flowed, the conversation had been easy, and she was happy. He was so affable and easy to talk to, she found herself opening up to him, telling him her life story. Even after the meal had arrived, she hardly ate from how much they spoke. From how the neighbor's dog had bitten her as a kid to her romantic foibles in high school, she told him story after story. After half an hour, she realised that she had been dominating the conversation with her anecdotes and pressed him for story about himself. He acquiesced and in turn told her how he had been dared to eat dog food as a child by his friends, and how he had actually gone through with it.

"That's disgusting!" Desirée laughed, "How did it taste?"

"It was rough, no pun intended," he flashed a smile, and Desirée found herself giggling and turning red. She grabbed her wine glass and drank some to hide her flushing face. She composed herself. "You have such a good grasp of English! I don't know if I'd be able to ever be as good as you are in another language."

"In my field, it's important to be able to speak multiple languages fluently. It makes it easier to get around and gather information."

"That makes sense to me, how is the journalism business these days?"

"Tiring, it can be difficult time pursuing the truth."

Desirée nodded, "I could see that."

"So, I hope I do not seem too eager to get down to business, but I was hoping I could ask you about some of your recent travels for my article," he inquired.

"Of course, Santiago," she grinned. 'This wine is getting to my head a bit,' she thought.

"Do you mind if I record our conversation?"

"Record?"

"For the article, of course," he quickly added, "It's easier than taking down notes, and allows conversation to flow more naturally."

"Of course," Desirée agreed.

"So you come from the United States originally, yes?"

"I do. Originally, I'm from Michigan, but most recently I'm from New York."

"Ah, New York is an amazing city. What is it that you do there?"

"I'm an actress. Stage only, I never had much patience for those Hollywood types. Much too arrogant and self-important."

Santiago laughed, as if in agreement, "I can only imagine! So what brings you to Marzine? Work or pleasure?"

Desirée feeling emboldened by the wine, locked eyes with Santiago, "Pleasure."

Diego felt his heart pulsing in his neck. He

had to stay focused, despite Desirée's flirtation. He continued his interrogation, "A nice holiday! Is this the only stop you've had so far?"

"No, I landed in Paris a little over a month ago. It was a wonderful time in Paris, I never thought that the city could live up to my dreams, and, yet, somehow it did. The whole trip so far has been amazingly wonderful, although, I *did* have quite an unexpected layover."

Diego's ears pricked up, "Ah, I'm sorry, that can be quite the hassle. What happened?"

"Some sort of routing trouble. We ended up getting sent to Athens for a mindbogglingly long layover. Sixteen hours, *overnight.*" Diego felt his heart sink.

"That is quite unfortunate," he said quietly.

"It was, but thankfully they put me up in a hotel and I even got to make some stops at some museums before the flight the next day. It may be boring, but I love museums," she laughed. "Finally, I made it to Paris in one piece and, as I said, I had the time of my life there."

If she had been at the museum a month ago… he pressed forward, and rallied himself, "And how was the trip from Paris coming here?"

"It was fine, excepting the sudden stop on the way," she then added playfully, "I believe you would know something about that."

Diego was shocked and taken aback slightly. His mind flashed back to the train ride earlier that day, and remembered that he had seen a woman very like Desirée as he had pursued the only path the masked perpetrator could have taken. Of course! His mind ran through the manifest he had studied earlier, Desirée's ticket had her sitting in the compartment right next to Charlotte's.

"You had said there was no time to explain earlier, perhaps now you can?" she cooed. It was over, she was toying with him, obviously. She knew exactly who he was and what he was doing. The jig was up.

He stood. "Miss Woods, my name is Diego Salvador," he flashed his badge, "I'm a Special Agent of the Royal Spanish Service, and I'm working in co-operation with DGSE and Interpol to bring the thief, Le Renard, AKA Charlotte Mechant, to justice and to recover the stolen Corona real de España. I'm afraid I must detain you and bring you to a safe location for further questioning."

Chapter 3

Desirée's mouth went dry. Santiago was NOT a journalist. Santiago wasn't even Santiago. Her mind was racing a million miles an hour, how could he think that she was this jewel thief, or even related to this thief?

"Miss Woods, you can come with me quietly or I can handcuff you. I would prefer for you to come quietly, as to avoid tipping off your partner to my presence here."

Partner? What was Santiago, no, scratch that, Diego talking about?

"I'm confused, what crime am I being accused of?"

"Aiding and abetting Charlotte Mechant, alias Le Renard, in the theft of one of Picasso's works in Athens, a month ago, and potentially the theft of the crown jewels of Spain."

Charlotte was involved in this? She was young and arrogant, surely, but currently the most wanted thief in the world? She couldn't believe it.

"Miss Woods. If you would please." Diego gestured for her to follow. Desirée had no choice, she stood and followed the newly christened Diego,

Spanish Special Agent. She continued following him through the lobby to the elevator. She stood behind him as the door opened and he motioned for her to enter first. Soon she found herself standing in front of a room door on the third floor. Diego opened it, "Follow me, please."

'So polite,' she thought bitingly. Once inside, she was greeted by a double room that was set up like a television crime show. The beds were pushed over to the side, with a desk set up in the middle. One chair on the side closest to her, and two chairs on the opposite side, one of which was occupied by a handsome man, who seemed in his late 50s.

"If you would do me the honor of sitting, mademoiselle," the older man spoke kindly in a thick French accent. She found herself being guided to her chair by Diego. Once she was sat, Diego sat opposite her, next to the other man. "My name is Jacques du Lac, I am a Senior Agent for the DGSE." He gestured to his right, "I believe you've already met Diego Salvador."

"I have," Desirée replied. She then shot a venomous look at Diego, "Or so I thought."

Diego's cheeks reddened slightly, "I would apologise, however, I believe that as an art thief, you have very little ground to stand on."

Desirée was insulted. She was supposed to be on vacation, and somehow she was now accused of being a criminal. This would not stand. "Well, Mr. Salvador, perhaps you should reconsider your stance, since I've never so much as stolen a penny in my life. You said I aided and abetted Le Renard? What proof do you have? That I was in Athens last month? I just saw about that on the news, earlier this evening. The museum was already closed because of the theft when I arrived! You never even asked me what specific day I was there!" Diego began to open his mouth, but Desirée cut him off, "and for your information, I had never met Charlotte before today! And, quite frankly, she seems too vapid to me to be this Le Renard of whom you speak!" She felt the blood rising to her ears now, "Maybe if you were better at your job, you wouldn't have dragged me up here for no reason!" Her chest was heaving with each breath. She saw Jacques lean over and whisper something softly into Diego's ear.

The two men stood up, Jacques saying, "Please don't leave, if you would give us just a moment, Mademoiselle." They then walked out to the balcony on the far end of the room and shut the doors behind them.

"You didn't ask for the specific day she was in Athens?" Jacques' face was stone.

"Well, no. I didn't. There were so many signs though!" Diego replied earnestly.

Jacques sighed, "Perhaps, but you may have also blown your cover for no reason. This was a beginner's mistake Diego."

"You think I don't know that?"

"Of course, I do, but I also know your history…"

Diego rounded on the graying man, "What do you know about my history? What dossier could you have read that could possibly explain what I've been through?"

"Diego, we've all had cases where we've made mistakes. That isn't an indictment on you, this is just life."

"Do your failed cases haunt you in your sleep, Jacques? Do you see their faces in your nightmares?"

Jacques put a compassionate hand on Diego's shoulder, "I wish I did not."

Diego didn't want to talk any further. He shook Jacques' hand away from his shoulder, "Let's focus on this case. Maybe Desirée isn't an accomplice, but she may know something that might help with trapping Charlotte. If we're lucky, Charlotte still has the stolen items within easy reach."

Jacques smiled sadly, "Let's see what we can do."

The two men reentered the room to see Desirée watching the television. "Not sorry," she stayed facing the program, "I didn't know how long you would be out there and I was bored."

"This is not a problem," Jacques answered. Diego stood there silently. Jacques hit him in the arm, and looked at him with disapproval.

Diego sighed, and looked sheepishly at Desirée. "I apologize for my presumptions and accusations, Desirée. I am eager to find a lead to this case, and every time I come close, Le Renard manages to elude me. We have worked long and hard on this case, and we are nearly 100% certain that Charlotte is Le Renard, regardless of appearances. I'm sure as an actress you know that they can be deceiving. You are the first person we've met who has spoken to Charlotte for any length of time. I was actually hoping that you would be willing to help me... please," he pleaded.

At his apology, Desirée's eyes finally left the program and turned to rest squarely on him, seemingly weighing everything that was going on, "What do you need me to do?"

Diego felt his heart jump, and renewed vigor in his spirit, "I'll need you to tell me everything you've learned about Charlotte Mechant."

"Well, that's quite a lot, as Charlotte very rarely shuts her mouth."

Diego smiled, this might have been the break he was waiting for. He sat down next to her, pulling out the recorder again, "Whenever you're ready."

Desirée spent the next twenty minutes pouring out everything she could recall from Charlotte's ramblings that day, "The last thing I can think of is that Charlotte had invited me to go skiing." She then sat back.

Diego perked up at this, "Did she give a specific time or place for the skiing?"

"She said tomorrow morning at 8. Apparently, she has an aunt or uncle who owns a house up on one of the mountains nearby. They have a private ski slope set up for fun. Charlotte offered to teach me. I actually have the address up in my room."

"This is perfect, Desirée!" Diego smiled broadly.

Jacques interrupted, "Miss Woods, we do not wish to place you in any danger, but it may be beneficial for us if you were to take Charlotte up on her offer. This will give Diego time to search the cabin for the stolen artifacts. It would be a great service to the entire world."

Desirée leapt to her feet, "Of course, I'll do it!"

"Meet me here at 6 tomorrow morning," Diego had a fire in his eyes, "we are going to catch the fox in the henhouse."

Chapter 4

Desirée had woken up at 5:30, if you could call it waking up. She hadn't been able to sleep the entire night, she was too excited. She had played all sorts of characters throughout her decades-long career, but this was a chance to do something incredibly dangerous for real, and it made her head spin. Adrenaline was surging out of every pore, and she knew that this was one of those moments in a life where you'd spend the rest of your days regretting not saying yes. She got dressed and ready quickly, and opted for the stairs to Diego's room, on the off chance that she might run into Charlotte in the elevator. There was no one.

She got to the room and knocked lightly, she was a little early, but not by much. The door opened and Diego brought her inside.

"You ready?" he asked.

"Never more so," she grinned.

"Take this and put it in your ear," Jacques was standing behind Diego with a tiny black earpiece, "it will allow you to hear us and stay in contact with us during the operation. You must be ready to follow any commands I give you. That goes for you, as well Diego," he shot a look at the younger man.

"Si, I understand, do not worry, all will be well!" Diego laughed. Desirée was shocked to see this change in Diego, yesterday he was dark and focused, but now he seemed lighter and looser, almost like a new person. The fire in his eyes hadn't dimmed, and only seemed to have grown brighter and greater. "Come Desirée, vamos!" He held open the door, and extended his hand. Desirée caught her breath, grabbed onto his hand and left the hotel with him.

It was still night out as they made their way through the silent town. Diego had let go of her hand soon after leaving the room, but she could still feel the strength of his fingers in hers. The street lamps reflected off the snow making a mockery of the dark, and she could see every detail of Diego's face in the soft light. He was younger than her, but she could see that he had more than a few white hairs. The curve of his jaw led to his lips, which were fuller than any man's had any right to be. His nose was well-proportioned to his face and was flanked by high, defined cheekbones. She noticed he hadn't shaved this morning, as he had a beard made out of slight stubble. She was impressed by his eyebrows, and slightly annoyed, 'were they naturally perfect like that, or does he do them?' she questioned internally. His hair fell in tight short curls. Just the right amount. He really was a very, very beautiful man. She let out a breath of steam in the chilly winter air and kept on creating footprints in the snow with the Spaniard.

They arrived at the edge of the town when Diego stopped, "Here is where we must go off the beaten path. We cannot have any tracks tipping off Charlotte that anyone has been here. We will do some reconnaissance on the cabin, and then you will return the way we came, and make it up to the cabin by the road," he pointed.

"Understood," Desirée nodded.

"Good, let us go."

They veered off to the right and trudged through the darkened forest. They arrived to the lookout point above the cabin far faster than Desirée had anticipated. She watched as Diego pulled out surveillance equipment. He had been silent nearly the whole time. Desirée was curious about him though. She realised that even during their dinner the previous night, Diego hadn't given a sliver of any information about Santiago, let alone himself.

"You seem like you know what you're doing," she remarked.

Diego was peering through a camera that he had set up on a tripod, "After fifteen years, I would hope that I had become at least slightly proficient."

"Have you had many missions like this?"

"I've had many operations, but like this? No."

"How did you get involved in all this to begin with?"

"The way anyone anywhere does. I was intelligent, athletic, and proficient at languages. I was approached shortly before my graduation from university, with an offer." He chuckled dryly, "They sell you on your patriotism, your belief in law and justice and the right." He turned to look at Desirée, "They tell you that you can make a difference, but..." Diego's face darkened and he looked down, "the truth is far more complicated than that."

Desirée felt slightly guilty, "I'm sorry if I hit on something..."

Diego's face turned up and his eyes met hers again, "Do not worry. I have done much good in my time as an agent."

"It sounds like there is an unspoken 'but' behind that."

"You're right. *But* we do not have time to continue speaking about this, as you need to return to the town to get ready to meet with Charlotte."

Desirée pursed her lips, he was right but she felt like she was within inches of discovering something about Diego. "I understand, I'll head back now."

Diego nodded, "Good. Remember, we can hear everything that you or Charlotte will say, and you will be able to hear both Jacques and I. Isn't that right, Jacques?"

"Oui, mes amis," came Jacques' disembodied voice from her ear piece. With that Desirée turned and followed the tracks they had made back to town.

"I'm back," Desirée spoke to no one in particular.

"Perfect," said Jacques, "You are clear to proceed to Charlotte's cabin. Remember that Diego has his eyes on you. He'll make sure you're alright."

Desirée began her walk up the path beside the road to where the cabin lay in wait. Her heart was pounding with each step she took towards the building. The path of the road was easier than the one to the vantage point earlier in the morning. She was thankful for her workout routine right about now. She hadn't seen a gym in a while, but her legs were doing fine with all the hills she had encountered that morning already, let alone when she was about to have to ski soon. She had never skied before, 'but that could be helpful,' she considered, 'it will serve to keep Charlotte out of the cabin longer.' She reached the turnoff for the cabin, and after a little more walking was greeted by the log building she had seen earlier from on high. She took a second to ready herself. It was rather cute, with a porch, a door in the middle and a window on either side of it.

"Good luck," Diego's voice whispered in her ear.

With that, Desirée strode determinedly to the door, and knocked strongly. There was no response. She knocked again. Again, no response. She checked her watch, it was 8am on the dot. She knocked one last time for good measure, and when there was no response, she decided to look into one of the windows. It was dark in there, as if no one had been there for quite sometime.

"I don't think Charlotte is here."
"Are you sure?" Jacques asked.

"I'm very sure. It's dark inside, and it doesn't look lived in at all."

"This is odd," Jacques mused, "Diego, you are clear to proceed down the hill and join Desirée."

Desirée heard a quiet rustling coming from somewhere behind the cabin, and more than a few choice words in Spanish came through her earpiece, but before long Diego was standing next to her, peering into the cabin as well.

"Jacques, do I have the go ahead to enter?" Diego inquired.

"Oui. I have verified that the cabin does belong to Mechant's family. You should be fine."

Diego turned to Desirée, "Are you ready?"

Desirée's heart was going a million miles a minute, "Absolutely."

Diego took out a small tool and walked towards the door, and began to fiddle around with the knob. With a small click, they were in. "Wait here," Diego, entered first, and then called out, "It's safe. You can come in."

Desirée entered the cabin and was surprised. It was almost all one large inset room, like a studio apartment. There was one door towards the back that she assumed opened into a bathroom. There were two long steps that ran the length of the cabin that led her down into the space. There was a small kitchen set up along the wall to her left, with oven and range, cabinets, and a dishwasher. To her right was a small TV nook, with some very comfortable looking chairs. Dead center in the room was an open air fireplace, with the chimney suspended above it. Behind that was a king sized bed.

"Jacques we're going radio dark, things are under control here."

"Understood."

"Go ahead and turn off your earpiece," Diego said to Desirée, as he did the same. "She may have stashed something here," said Diego to her left. He was looking through, the cabinets. "Look for anything out of place." Desirée walked around finding nothing until she had reached the opposite side of the cabin. She checked the drawer of the bedside table closest to her. There was a bible and a new box of condoms in it. 'Slightly odd,' she thought to herself. She moved on, checking the right side of the bed when she noticed what looked like a piece of paper underneath one of the pillows. She reached for it and pulled out an envelope with her name on it. "Diego, I've found something!"

Diego rushed over, "What is it?"

"It's a letter for me?"

"Well, that's certainly out of place. Go ahead and open it," he urged.

Desirée opened the letter and read it out loud.

My dearest Desirée,

I'm sorry that it's come to this. I really do like you, you know. You quite possibly are the most unique person I've ever met. It may sound cliché but it's not you, it's me. You can inform your Spanish friend, that MY jewels are safely in my possession, and that I took the first train out of town this morning. I forget, did I ever tell you what I went to university for in the United States? It was chemistry. Do you know how easy it is to rig an explosive? Don't worry, I'm not going to kill you. Like I said, I like you Desirée. But, I can't have you following me either. Fortunately for both of us, the cabin that you're in was reinforced in case of avalanche.

Love, Charlotte

Diego and Desirée's eyes met in mutual understanding, as they heard an explosion, somewhere on the mountain above them. Desirée began to run to the door, when Diego grabbed her arm, "There's not enough time!" He then grabbed her and held her close as the rumbling grew louder and louder. It sounded like a freight train was barreling towards them. Suddenly, all the windows darkened as hundreds of tons of snow flew past the windows. They heard snow landing on the roof, and heard the cabin groan under the pressure.

Finally, after what seemed an eternity, the roar died down. It was pitch black now. Diego let go of Desirée. She heard him fumbling for something, then there was a *pfft* as he flicked a lighter on. The soft glow of the flame extended a few feet around them, "Give me a moment." He got up, and she saw the tiny flame grow smaller as Diego walked away from her. "Luckily, it looks like the snow didn't cover the top of the chimney," he remarked, "I should be able to light a fire safely." True to his word, a few minutes later he had a small fire going in the fireplace, and there was enough light to see the room by. They took off their wet jackets, socks, and snow boots to dry and seated themselves on the ground next to the fire.

"Do you think that Jacques knows we're stuck?" Desirée asked.

"If he doesn't now he will soon. Avalanches are serious issues, but they are a known quantity."

"Why don't we try the earpieces? Maybe we can reach him."

"First thing I tried. There was only static when I turned mine on."

"Well, how long will we be here?"

"Depending on the nature of the avalanche and how quickly teams get mobilized, a few hours to a few days, but I'm going to say that in our situation, at least a day or so," Diego seemed very tired suddenly. "I failed again," came the whisper from his lips.

"What do you mean?" Desirée tilted her head confused.

"I don't want to talk about it." Diego's response was sharp.

It stung. "I'm sorry, I didn't mean to upset you."

Diego sighed and his shoulders slumped. He drew his legs close to his chest and wrapped them with his arms, "No. I'm sorry. I shouldn't have snapped. It's not your fault." He looked at her with glistening eyes.

Desirée inched closer to him, and put her hand on his knee, "You don't have to talk about it if you don't want, but I'm willing to listen."

Diego's glistening eyes turned to silent tears, "It's not a fun story, it's not nice. It's painful for me to tell it."

"Like I said, only if you want to."

Diego turned and looked at the fire for a while. "Why the hell not. We're stuck here anyway."

Desirée braced herself as Diego began his story.

"What's the best way to begin?" In truth, he didn't know himself, so he decided to just start at the beginning. "I was a newly graduated agent, and it was my first command assignment. I was confident, and thought like many young men do, that I was immortal. That I could do no wrong, and that I was some great hero that was going to save the world. I didn't know how incorrect I was.

"There was a scientist that had gone rogue, and had stolen top-secret files from the central government. He had been captured, but had initiated a two hour countdown that would send the information to unscrupulous parties and rogue states. Desirée, this information was highly dangerous. If the wrong people got their hands on it, it could have potentially meant the deaths of millions of people. We had been searching for where the file transmission was going to take place and found it with an hour left. It was an old estate in the Spanish countryside. My team and I arrived with ten minutes to spare. Unfortunately, with so little time, we didn't have the luxury of doing a sweep to find the transmission apparatus. I called into my superiors to ask for their orders, they told me that the scientist had informed them that the building was empty and he had been staying there alone. I was ordered to set off explosives we had brought, and to obliterate the building and everything inside.

"I did as I was told. I wired the explosives in the main hall which was central to the building. This took time, and we were down to the last two minutes before it would be too late. I ran out the building to the designated safe zone that my men had set up. The seconds were counting down. With thirty seconds left, I was given the all clear. Something didn't feel right to me. I couldn't put my finger on what it was, but something was off. I hesitated for a moment, but I decided to press the button anyway. I looked up as I pressed it to see a little girl standing in a second story window, her hand on the glass. Her face disappeared when she was engulfed in the flames of the explosives.

"As it turns out, my superiors *knew* that the scientist's daughter was in the house. He had told them so, but they decided that there wasn't enough time to find her, and that her death was a fair exchange for preventing the information from escaping. They even gave me an award and told me that I had done what was right for the world."

He felt the hot tears rising in his eyes, and a yell erupted from his throat, "THE BASTARDS KNEW!" Diego broke down sobbing, "I see her face every night. I should have known. I should have been better. I had time to check, I could have found her," he was rambling. "I swore after that, that I would be perfect from then on. I wouldn't make any mistakes, I wouldn't have any slip ups..." his voice trailed off into tears. He felt Desirée's hand on his cheek, and her voice was soft, "From what you told me, it wasn't your fault Diego. You can't blame yourself for what happened."

Diego wanted to pull away from Desirée, but found himself being drawn in. Desirée put her arms around him and held him close, "It's alright Diego, you're a good person. It's not your fault."

"I've never told anyone that story," Diego murmured.

"I appreciate being the first one to hear it," Desirée said gently. "You know, I haven't talked to anyone about it since it happened, but I understand feeling like you should have been able to do more. I lost my mother when I was six, and for years I felt like it was my fault."

"What happened?"

"My mother and I were playing hide and seek, and it was my turn to hide, so I went to my favorite hiding place, and hid in the closet in my room. I heard my mom yell, 'ready or not here, I come,' and that was it. I hid and waited for her to find me, minutes passed by and I was feeling proud of myself, but slowly those minutes passed, and it was dark in the closet. I ended up falling asleep, and only woke up when I heard my father yelling my name in my room. I got up immediately, because there was something wrong in his voice. He immediately grabbed me and held on to me, asking if I were okay. I didn't understand what was going on or what had happened. I told him that I was okay, and that I was playing hide and seek with Mommy. He told me that Mommy was being taken care of in an ambulance on the way to the hospital. She had had something bad happen to her and that we needed to go check on her at the hospital.

"As it turned out, she had a heart attack not long after I hid. She had lain there for several hours while I was asleep in the closet. My father had found her and immediately called the emergency services. She was dead before she arrived at the hospital. As I got older, I learned that if she had gotten to the hospital sooner, she probably would have lived, but I was hiding and she was just laying there helpless."

Diego looked at Desirée, "That's not your fault. How could that be your fault, you were only a child, and what happened was a tragedy, but it was an accident."

"I know, but I'm sure you can understand, that it's not always that simple."

Diego brushed her hair out of her face, petting her head, and hugged her close to him. He felt

Desirée adjusting him and holding him closer. He looked up into her eyes. They were beautiful- she was beautiful. Diego sat up out of her arms, and placed his hand on her cheek. Her eyes twinkled in the fire light. He found himself being drawn to her lips. It may have been the adrenaline from surviving the avalanche, it may have been the emotional release from having shared intimate stories. He didn't know, and he didn't care. He just knew he wanted one thing in that moment, and that was Desirée.

Desirée felt Diego lean closer to her face and felt a magnetic pull towards him.

"Would you mind terribly if I kissed you?" he asked, his lips hovering above hers.

"I thought you'd never ask," whispered Desirée. Diego took her consent and lightly brushed his lips against hers before committing to a deep, passionate embrace, their bodies pressed tightly against one another. She felt his strong hands on her back, one between her shoulder blades, and another in the small. Her heart was pounding in her ears, she could hear her blood rushing, and feel it flowing downwards. She wanted this man, very badly. Diego started kissing her neck, and she could feel the caress of his rough beard. It would probably leave a mark, but she didn't care, she wanted him to take her. She took his hands, which had been very polite so far, and moved them further down to her firm cheeks. Diego took the hint and gave a squeeze, and started nibbling on her ear. She shuddered as he did so. She could hear his heavy breath, hot in her ear. She felt her own breathing rapidly increase. His fingers had begun tracing the outline of her sides, down to her legs. A feather's touch would have been heavier, and she could feel goosebumps rising.

"You can touch me anywhere," Desirée breathed.

"Are you sure?" Diego asked between neck kisses.

"Absolutely," she moaned. Desirée felt Diego's hands entering her shirt, and she felt his hands going to her bra to unclasp it. When it came undone, Diego lifted her shirt off, and Desirée let her bra slide off. Diego stopped for a short moment to admire Desirée, "You are magnificent." Desirée would have blushed, or returned the favor if Diego hadn't proceeded to take off his shirt. Shirtless, he was well muscled with a lightly defined six pack, and his smile was clear in the firelight, "I figured it's only fair." He reached out to bring her closer to him, and she felt herself yielding to his strong and powerful frame. He leaned her back and began kissing her chest and stomach, lightly teasing her nipples with his tongue. Her body felt electric and alive. She began to ache as he explored her body. She shuddered as his breath washed over her sides, as he was kissing her. His hands finally found their way to her pants. She felt her heart nearly explode as his hands entered. She felt pleasure start to wash over her and through her as they explored between her thighs, playing with her wetness. Desirée wanted, no, *needed* this man. She reached for his body and felt his rough-hewn muscle under her grasping fingertips. She copied his lines, starting at his round, broad shoulders, and following the downward v of his body to his expansive chest, before reaching his abs. She traced them, feeling the strength within them. Diego laid her down, "Do you want to keep going?"

Desirée did, but was suddenly concerned with the lack of protection, before she remembered the drawer with the bible and the condoms, "There's a package of condoms in the bedside table."

"Sounds good," he smiled. In a flash, Diego was back to kissing her. She felt his hands grabbing the waistband of her pants and pulling them down her legs. Soon she was lying on the floor, bathed in nothing but shadows and firelight. Diego sat above her, he reached down and picked her up. She felt safe in his arms as she put hers around his neck. He bent his face towards hers and kissed her. She melted as he carried her towards the bed. He laid her down softly on the edge of the bed, her legs hanging over the side. He started kissing her body again and Desirée leaned back in delight. Diego moved further down and started kissing the insides of her thighs while his hands lightly flowed over her legs. Desirée gasped aloud and clutched the comforter when Diego's kisses found her pussy, and she felt his tongue running over and in it. He stayed down there for a few minutes, tasting her, before he came back up and kissed her again. She wanted him inside of her now. She sat up, and grabbed his pants.

She unbuttoned the top, and let them fall down. She could see his hard cock pressing against the front of his boxer briefs, straining to get out. She decided to free it. She leaned back to admire her handiwork: a caramel Diego standing in the flickering light, hard in every way. His legs were thick and strong, and he looked every inch like of piece of renaissance art. "I want you," Desirée commanded, locking eyes with Diego. Diego, reached over for a condom, and soon was wearing it while leaning over her. She trembled as his package slowly entered her. She felt him push inside her. He groaned with pleasure above her. He started rotating his hips around, and began taking her more forcefully. Desirée was crying out with pleasure. Diego moaned, "You're so sexy, Desirée."

As his manhood plunged in and out of Desirée, Diego looked into her eyes. She saw a light in them that spoke in hushed tones of devotion and longing. "You're beautiful," he said simply. Desirée pushed Diego off and onto his back. She got on top of him and took his hard rod in her hand and guided him in. She wanted to give Diego pleasure like he had given her. She put both of her hands on his chest and began to ride him, causing him to moan in ecstasy. She started going harder and harder, the headboard of the bed hitting into the wall again and again, Diego started to get louder. Desirée felt his throbbing cock hard inside of her as drove herself increasingly mad with heat. The headboard began slamming into the wall as Diego began to cry out in pleasure with each new bounce. Desirée's body was slick with sweat and she could feel Diego's heart racing underneath her hands.

"I need you!" Diego cried out as he added his own thrusting to hers. They locked together in sync, the bed creaking below them, the headboard slamming into the wall, and their cries of passion coming to a crescendo. Desirée felt wave after wave of pleasure as she finally came, Diego still thrusting into her, causing her legs to quiver and nearly give out from the pleasure. Diego grabbed her hips firmly and kept thrusting, harder and harder, again and again. Finally, with one last thrust, he pushed himself deep into her, and shuddered, breathing heavily in her ear as he hugged her tightly to him, their bodies entwining like vines. They held each other for what seemed like an eternity in a single moment, but finally, Diego withdrew himself from within her. They locked eyes, and kissed again, a slow, lingering, passionate kiss. Desirée pulled back smiling from the act, her hair falling in front of her eyes.

"Did you become this proficient with 15 years of experience, too?" she joked.

"Actually, no," he admitted, brushing her hair out of her face, "I must say, I'm actually not all that experienced with this. Not a lot of time for romance, when your constantly on international duty, and you don't know who might be trying to shoot you. Makes it hard to trust people."

"I understand, not with being shot at, obviously, but I was left with a lot of alone time, too. I never knew when my next gig was, and in the acting world it can be difficult to know who likes you for you, and who likes you for what you can do for them. It's really lonely."

"It is," Diego agreed. He paused. "You know..." he started.

"Yes?"

"I trust you."

Desirée beamed, "I trust you too."

Diego smiled back, "What should we do now?"

Desirée, looked down and back up at him, "You think there's any food in here?"

Chapter 5

It was a fairly uneventful day after the initial excitement and the avalanche. It was that evening when Desirée and Diego heard people calling down the chimney to check if they were alright. When they confirmed that they were, they were told that the ETA for getting them out was going to be the next morning.

Diego was pacing; frustrated that the trail was going to continue growing colder with each passing minute. Charlotte was going to get away with the jewels, the Picasso, and who knew what else. He turned his head to look over at Desirée. She was laying on the bed, taking a nap. He cracked a slight smile while looking at her. She was wonderful and he found that they had a lot more in common than he would have guessed. After some of the stories she had told him about the men in the acting world, he was thankful he only ever had to worry about people shooting at him. 'Or send avalanches my way,' he thought dryly. His thoughts returned to Charlotte. He had to figure out how she had known he and Desirée were there. He ran over her file again in his head. She was highly intelligent and capable.

Rigging a bomb to set off an avalanche? Impressive, to say the least. She also had evaded several guards by climbing through ventilation shafts. In order to avoid making any noise the agency believed that she had taken two days to travel the entire length. He shook his head. That kind of patience, focus, and endurance was insane. She couldn't be going anywhere in the world, not with what she was carrying, but she could easily go almost anywhere in Europe. Crossing national borders would be simple for her, and much more difficult for him. His agency would have to get into contact with Interpol again, and they'd have to get authorization from whatever the intelligence or policing agencies along Charlotte's chosen escape route would be. There weren't any options. They had to prevent her from leaving France.

Desirée startled Diego out of his train of thoughts by stirring in the bed. She sat up, yawning and stretching. "I had a dream that Charlotte lied to us," she said bleary eyed.

Diego laughed mirthlessly, "Very imaginative."

"No, that's not what I meant."

"What did you mean?" he asked.

"What if she didn't leave by train at all? Why would she tell us that?"

Diego was taken aback slightly, "Go on."

"Everything in the note seemed truthful, right? I mean, she seemed sincere, and she did cause an avalanche."

"Right…"

"*So*, what if she lied at the end, knowing that we'd be primed to believe her?"

Diego sat next to the fire rubbing his light beard, "You know, you're absolutely right. The only train out of this town goes straight to Paris, and takes too long. She would have tipped her hand with the avalanche and Jacques would have men stationed waiting for her arrival."

"Exactly," Desirée agreed.

"Then she hasn't left the town most likely. And as this proves," he gestured to the cabin around them, "she's spent ample time in this place. We're on her ground and she knows the terrain."

"Then we'll have to think fast if we're going to catch her."

Diego shook his head, "Desirée, I appreciate your help with all of this, but your part must be done. I can't risk you any further, you're a civilian."

Desirée mouth opened in disbelief. "I can't believe you!" She was angry, and Diego was going to know it.

"What do you mean?" He seemed confused.

"I've risked my life to help you, and even made you rethink where Charlotte may have gone, and you're just going to throw me away. No. It's not happening."

"Desirée, be reasonable. You've been helpful, but I can't justify taking you along in this case."

"Diego, I'm not leaving until this case is

through, and that's final. You do whatever you need to do to make that happen, but it's happening."

Diego rubbed his temples and was silent for a minute as Desirée shot daggers at him. Diego looked up and was about to speak when he saw her look, and closed his mouth again. Finally, he turned back to her, "I do technically have the power to deputize someone. It's not a permanent thing, but it would allow you to join me in the capacity of agent for the duration of the case."

"Do it."

"Done."

Desirée jumped into Diego's arms, and gave him a long kiss. He started laughing, "You know, you might just be crazy enough for this to work."

Desirée just smiled and gave him another kiss.

It was a few hours later when a bright light shone through one of the windows. Desirée tapped Diego on his arm, "Look." Diego jumped up and ran to the window, throwing it open. Desirée could see the rescuer dressed in orange. "Avez-vous besoin d'aide?" he asked in a joking manner. Diego smiled, "Merci beaucoup, oui!" Desirée got to her feet and went to grab her boots and jacket. A few minutes later they were crawling out of the cabin window into the frigid, dark night. There was an entire team of people working on excavating the house from under the tons of snow. Standing in the midst of all of it was Jacques, holding two cups of something.

"I'm glad to see both of you in one piece," he said tiredly. "I brought something for both of you." He handed both Desirée and Diego the cups. Desirée drank from it, and it was warmed by hot cocoa.

"What happened?" Jacques asked.

"Charlotte rigged explosives on the mountain above the cabin to snow us in," Diego explained.

"That is something," the older man responded.

"There have been several developments though that you should be aware of," Diego responded.

"Come, we can speak in the car on the way back to town, it is a very short drive." Jacques turned his back and began walking to a red car that was parked on the perimeter of the property. Diego and Desirée followed him, Desirée climbing into the back of the car while Diego got into the front passenger seat. Desirée felt the car rumble to life, and watched as Jacques turned the car on to the wintry road.

"So what are these developments?" Jacques asked.

"Firstly, I deputized Desirée so that she could continue helping with the case. She knows more about Charlotte than anyone else, and Charlotte apparently has some sort of fondness for her."

Jacques was unperturbed by this, "I see. How did you become aware of this fondness?"

"She left us a letter," Desirée replied, looking out the window as the car rolled back into the town.

"In the letter, she essentially said that she couldn't have us following her, but that she liked Desirée, so she wasn't going to kill us," Diego explained.

"Indeed, it's lucky you had Desirée with you then," Jacques laughed. "Was there anything else that the letter said?"

"She claimed that she left town this morning," Diego told him. The car came to a halt, in front of the hotel. They all got out, reentering the chilly night.

"I see," Jacques shook his head as they walked towards the hotel, "I do not believe she would have been able to elude the men stationed at the Paris station. After the avalanche this morning I sent immediate word to Paris."

"Exactly!" Desirée beamed at the men.

Jacques looked at her slightly confused, but Diego elaborated, "Desirée made the point that she only wanted us to think she left by train. Desirée even said you would have had a team waiting for her when she arrived in Paris."

"That is true," Jacques agreed as they entered into the hotel lobby.

"Welcome back," Vincent the 19th called from his desk.

Diego and Jacques ignored him and were walking towards the elevators, but Desirée stopped.

"Wait a second," she told the men, but as they

turned she had already gone and walked over to the kindly old man, asking, "Monsieur Vincent, had you ever seen Charlotte Mechant before her stay here recently?"

Vincent smiled, "Of course! She comes here very often! Her family used to live here for a time, very close to mine. She was such a charming young girl. Her father was a historian who was researching the bunkers and tunnels that the Germans had built during the second World War. Quite tragic, actually, he ended up becoming rather mentally ill. He began to make ridiculous claims, and he had to be admitted to an asylum. They cured him eventually, but he passed away shortly after." He shook his head sadly, "Very tragic."

Diego and Jacques came closer as Desirée probed further, "There are bunkers and tunnels in Morzine?"

"Ah no, mademoiselle, not in the city proper, but up the mountain side, along the main road. It gave a vantage point over the town for the Nazis to watch the valley."

"Thank you very much, Vincent," Desirée smiled widely.

"Of course, mademoiselle," Vincent the 19th returned the smile.

Desirée turned around to the agents behind her, "You all heard the man, you know where our next stop is. We need to go now."

"I admire your tenacity and fearlessness, but you cannot be certain that Charlotte will not have

THE SPY IN THE ALPS

laid another surprise," Jacques reminded her.

"He is right," Diego agreed, "We need to make sure that we're not going to waltz into another trap again."

Desirée shook her head, "No. You forget I'm the only person who's met her. She may have fooled me into thinking she wasn't as smart as she was. She is supremely confident, however, and faked or not, that level of confidence only comes if you think that you're always one step ahead. I don't think she thought that we'd see through the letter."

"We don't know for sure that she was even lying in that letter, Desirée, we have to regroup first," Diego snapped.

Desirée was taken aback. She looked at Diego, then to Jacques in askance, then back to Diego. She knew she was right, but they were going to try to stop her if she told them so. "You're right," she lied, "I'm tired anyway, I'll see you both in the morning?"

Diego smiled, seemingly relieved, "Absolutely. Get some rest."

"Bonne nuit," Jacques lightly bowed his head.

Desirée took the elevator with the men to their floor, and then to hers. She then pressed the button for the lobby. Each floor seemed to inch by, her heart pounding out of fear of being discovered. The elevator was approaching Diego and Jacques' floor. It stopped. Her heart did too. The door opened and Diego was standing there. He laughed, "Well, you didn't think I was going to let you go alone did you? You should see your face." He walked in, a pack on his back, and Desirée felt her face get red, so she punched him in the arm. "You should see your face," she mocked back at him her tongue hanging out of her mouth. The elevator arrived at the lobby. Diego walked out purposefully, saying, "We got a job to do."

Desirée felt déjà vu as they were walking through the darkened town like they had that the previous morning. She glanced over at Diego. He was quiet and looked very tired.

"How did you know I was going to go?" she asked.

"It's what I would have done, and honestly, I don't think I could have stopped you had I tried."

Desirée smiled halfheartedly, "Do you think Charlotte is going to be there?"

"I don't know, and quite frankly, there's a chance we're wrong."

"Do you think I'm wrong?"

"I think that it's impossible for me to say. One of the most important tools for any agent is to trust their gut," he paused for a moment, "I trust yours." He kept walking.

Desirée was quiet. Then she reached out and grabbed Diego's hand. He looked down at their hands, and gave hers a squeeze, and kept holding it. They continued their trek to the mountains, finally crossing into the woods. The empty tree branches reached grasping fingers up to the cloudless sky, which shown with thousands of glimmering stars.

The wind had died down and there was a hush in the air, as if the world was afraid to take a breath. The silence was only broken by their footsteps crunching through the deep snow. Desirée began to feel nervous, and wondered silently if they were making the right choice. She tried to reassure herself, surely, Charlotte couldn't be that dangerous. If she wanted to hurt or kill anyone, she could have done so with the avalanche, and she didn't.

As if sensing her unease, Diego gave her hand a squeeze, "It's going to be alright. I've been in far more dangerous situations than this, and we'll be fine." Desirée nodded in agreement, but was unable to shake the feeling.

It was a few hours later when they found the entrance to the bunker off the side of the road. It was in an old clearing and was boarded up with signs in French warning of danger and to stay away. There was a large door with broken cement leading to it that had clearly once served as an entrance for military vehicles, and to the right, next to it, up a small set of stairs was another smaller door for individuals to enter. She watched Diego walk up to the door, took of his backpack and knelt to open it. He took out a flashlight, and shined it along the edges of the door.

"The door is rusted over, but the hinges are clean, someone's been here recently," he stated matter-of-factly.

"I knew it!" Desirée whispered excitedly.

"All we know is someone's been here. We

don't know who," Diego reminded her. "But, I'm thinking you might be right… we may have found her." He gestured with the flashlight, "Come on, let's get inside."

Desirée followed Diego's path to the door as he opened it. It glided with ease. Desirée felt vindicated. She entered behind Diego into a large access tunnel. The door they had come in through was for a raised pathway that ran alongside the tunnel. Diego held up the flashlight, and shined it around. The concrete walls of the tunnel were dripping water and cracking in places, but seemed strong enough.

"There's another flashlight in my bag, Desirée, go ahead and grab it."

Desirée unzipped the backpack and felt around in it until she found it. She pulled it out and flicked it on. Light poured out in front of her. She shined the light on the wall nearest her. There was an old faded sign in German. It read, 'Achtung! Militärische Einrichtung. Betreten verboten!' She assumed it was warning not to enter.

"Vamos!"

She looked at the source of the voice and saw Diego's flashlight receding from her. She ran to catch up, "That was rude."

"We can go sightseeing later, we need to stay focused on the task ahead."

"Fine."

They followed along the tunnel as it curved inside the mountain. Time seemed to go on forever, as they walked, the tunnel seemingly extending into infinity.

"Do you think this tunnel is ever going to end?" Desirée asked exasperatedly, she had to admit, she was getting tired. "Maybe we can-"

"Shh!" Diego cut her off. He pointed ahead to a faint light. Diego looked at her pointed to her then his flashlight, and turned his off. She got the message and did the same. Diego's hand gripped her suddenly in the darkness and he pulled her forward towards the light. Slowly, the encroaching light grew larger and larger in the encompassing darkness. As they inched closer, they were able to make out details in the light. It was coming from a very large room, easily tens of feet tall, and long enough that they couldn't see the far end of the room from their vantage point. They came to the edge of the entrance. Diego signaled for Desirée to stand back. Her hands were shaking, but she steadied herself. She wanted to be ready for whatever was coming.

CLICK

In an instant, Diego and Desirée were bathed in fluorescent light.

A woman's voice deeper than Charlotte's came booming from nowhere and everywhere, "Welcome Desirée! I'm so glad you could make it!" Desirée looked around for the source, but couldn't find it. "You brought a plus one! That is so sweet, you know, you two make an adorable couple, please come into my great hall!" Desirée looked at Diego who seemed just as shocked as she was. He held out his hand to her. Desirée ran to him. "Don't worry," came the voice again almost cooing, "you are perfectly safe here. You are my guest, and I am your humble host." Desirée and Diego looked at each other locking eyes. With a single mutual nod, they walked into the room hand in hand, utterly unprepared for what was coming next.

Chapter 6

Desirée and Diego were still squinting from the sudden shift in light when they entered the abandoned warehouse. It was empty of furniture, or anything really, save a single long table in the middle and two giant floor length tapestries at the end that both held some sort of royal crest. There was food on the end of the table closest to them with two chairs, and a single lit candelabrum as a center piece. On the far end was an identical set up, except, instead of a chair, there was a throne flanked by two men in medieval armor. Sitting in the throne, wearing the Crown of Spain, was none other than Charlotte Mechant.

"Please, sit, enjoy the meal!" she called. Desirée was shocked, her voice was deeper than it had been. Before she had sounded like a valley girl with a French accent, now she sounded much older, more refined, and dangerous.

"Thank you for such kindness, your majesty!" Diego bowed mockingly.

Charlotte laughed, "You jest and yet, I forgive you my faithful subject. You are loyal to the throne, and that is good and right. You simply don't know that the man sitting in it is a Pretender."

"How dare you!" Diego spat, "Juan Carlos is the one and rightful King!"

Charlotte rose in a fury, "That Bourbon Pretender sits on the throne of Trastámara!"

"The House of Trastámara is dead! It died hundreds of years ago!" Diego's chest was heaving, and anger flashed in his eyes.

Desirée was confused, she knew almost nothing of Spanish Politics and knew even less about what was happening here, "I'm sorry, what, exactly, is this argument about?"

Diego spoke without taking his eyes off of Charlotte, "She claims that the throne of Spain belongs to her, and she uses the name of the long dead as the justification," he raised his voice louder, "Even if there were any claim to the throne, the House of Trastámara has no living members!"

Charlotte sat back down silently as Diego's voice echoed and died out. She leaned back, kicking one of her legs over the armrest of her throne, "That is where you are wrong Diego. Tell me do you know of John of House Trastámara, Prince of Asturias?" She seemed to take Diego's furious silence as a no. "Let me enlighten you." She sat up, "John, Prince of Asturias, was born heir presumptive to Isabelle the First and Ferdinand the Fifth. As he grew up, this status made his older sister jealous. So jealous, in fact, that she decided that he should die. She knew that if John were out of the way, that she would be next in line to the throne. But you see, John was a good, trusting man, who could never imagine that his sister would commit herself to such acts of fratricide. His trusting nature was betrayed at her wedding. She poisoned him and he died a week later. His new widow, Margaret of Austria, was seven months pregnant. Margaret knew that her husband had been murdered, so she devised a plan to protect the child in her womb from the machinations of their aunt.

"The day of birthing came, and, to her great joy, she gave birth to a strong, healthy baby boy. She bribed the midwives, however, to take the child and to leave the room somberly, and to inform the waiting party that her daughter had died in labor. The child was smuggled safely out, and the boy lived.

"That boy was taken by his mother to Savoy under the guise of a child of one of her servants. He was secretly tutored, trained, and taught the truth of his heritage. His mother begged him out of the love that she bore for him to not try to reclaim the Spanish throne, but to live a good and Godly life. The boy had much of his father in him, and so he promised his mother that he would. He took a wife and began a new line, a royal line in exile. A line that was passed down from father to son for generations, until tragically, my father and brothers were taken from me by a plane crash. I swore then that the line of John wouldn't die, and that I would reclaim my family's rightful place on the throne."

Charlotte stood up, "I am the House Trastámara, Charlotte the First, rightful Queen of Spain." She looked down on Desirée and Diego with a cold fury, "And you shall not prevent me from claiming what is mine by Divine Right." She snapped her fingers, and the man to her right pulled a horn from his waist and blew on it, a single piercing note. Diego and Desirée stood motionless, as the sound of the horn faded away. Then from behind Charlotte came the sound of rushing footsteps, as men poured out from behind the tapestries. Unlike the men that flanked her, these were dressed in modern combat gear, and had the weapons to match.

Diego grabbed Desirée, "Run!" he yelled. It was too late though, they were surrounded.

"I invited you to enjoy the meal," Charlotte said. Desirée turned, Charlotte was walking on top of the table towards them now. "You refused my hospitality, you threaten me in my own home. Now, you try to run." She stopped suddenly and addressed the soldiers, her head tilted at an odd angle, "Was I a bad host? That simply won't do at all. How can you follow a Queen who doesn't take care of her subjects? Soldados, take our guests to their accommodations. Make sure they have every comfort. I won't stand for a single hair on their heads to be harmed." She turned away from Diego and Desirée, "Now I have to find a new base of operations. Tragic, really, but c'est la vie. Take them away."

Desirée was in shock as men took Diego's backpack, and handcuffed both of them. She looked at Diego who was being pushed towards the tapestries like she was. "What do we do?" she mouthed at him.

"Be patient," was his reply in kind.

The uniformed men escorted Desirée and Diego deeper into the labyrinthine innards of the mountain complex. Desirée's eyes grew wide as they passed room after room full of soldiers. How did Charlotte have such a following? There were easily thousands of men here from what she could see, and Charlotte was just an art thief! The realization hit her like a ton of bricks. Charlotte stole artwork worth millions, and she was funding an army with it. She took a glance over at Diego, who seemed to have reached the same conclusion. Suddenly, Diego winked at her. She looked at him confused and he looked at her with a look that told her to be quiet. Diego took a look around, and nudged a guy next to him. "So what's the going rate for an army of mercenaries these days?" he chimed jovially. The men ignored him. He continued slightly louder, "An operation like this must cost a lot of money. I mean, not just that but the logistics must be insane! Is she feeding you well? You're looking like skin and bones!" The men ignored him again. "I just can't imagine what sort of whores your mothers were that this was the best you could achieve with your lives." That got a reaction.

The man who had taken his backpack shoved him to the ground, and in an American southern accent yelled, "The fuck did you say about my mom?"

Diego smiled up at him, "I called her a whore."

The man snarled, "You motherfucker." He

went to backhand Diego, but was caught off guard when Diego ducked under his hand and swept his feet out from under him, knocking him out cold when his head smashed to the ground. Diego popped up, looking at the rest of the men who were standing there dumbfounded "That was unfortunate! Gentlemen, surely there's no need for such violence." The men stood for a moment and then they all rushed him. Diego shoved Desirée out of the way, still handcuffed, and proceeded to fight the men. The soldiers were yelling in different languages and accents as they struggled to get a single strike to find its mark. Desirée watched in astonishment as Diego weaved between punches and kicks, redirecting them onto the soldiers themselves. Slowly, one by one, Diego knocked out the soldiers, until finally he was standing alone in the middle of a ring of unconscious men.

"Diego that was incredible!"

He smiled, "You didn't think I was just a pretty face, did you? Come on, one of these guys must have keys that can unlock our cuffs." They fumbled around in the pockets of the men, until they found the keys. Moments later, the cuffs were unlocked and they were freed.

"What do we do now?" asked Desirée.

Diego was about to respond when he was interrupted by a shout from down the hall. It was another group of soldiers on patrol, and they began running and yelling at Diego and Desirée to stand and stay where they were.

"In answer to your question, I say we run," Diego said quietly to Desirée. Diego picked up his backpack where it had fallen. "Let's go!" He grabbed Desirée's hand and they bolted down the corridor as fast as they could leaving the scene behind. Behind them they could hear footsteps getting louder, so in an effort they began taking random turns in the catacomb-like tunnels. Left, right, right, left, all the turns in the torturous maze continued to get the more lost in the base, but kept them one step ahead of the chasing footsteps. Desirée noticed yellow tape along the entrance to a stairwell that was coming up to their right. She pulled on Diego and ducked into the darkened stairs. They pressed themselves in to the dark shadows and held their breath. Desirée's heart pounded ever louder in her ears as the following footsteps became louder and more pronounced. Her heart skipped several beats as the guards came into view, sprinting past the stairs. There were several of them, but they were gone in a flash, and soon their footsteps began to fade too. Neither Diego nor Desirée moved a muscle, waiting for the last sounds of footfalls to disappear. Finally, all was quiet, and they let out haggard breaths, clutching onto each other as adrenaline cascaded through their veins. Desirée looked up into Diego's eyes, she had never seen a more attractive pair in her life. She buried her face in his chest. She had never felt more alive than she did in that moment, the whole situation was exhilarating. Diego squeezed her closer, "Come on we need to figure out a place to lay low, and figure out our next step." They set off back down the hall, constantly on the look out for further soldiers and guards, but didn't come across any.

They reached the ending of a long hall with a single door. The door was old, with rusted hinges, and it looked like it hadn't been opened in a very long time. There was a sign on it in German, 'Offiziersquartier'.

"We might as well give it a shot," Diego shrugged.

"Sounds good to me," Desirée agreed.

Diego grabbed the handle and turned, shoving his shoulder into the door. It groaned under the pressure he applied. Not giving an inch, he pushed harder and harder trying to get the door to budge. Somewhere in the distance, a shout rose, Desirée's heart froze. Diego muttered something that sounded like a curse in Spanish, and threw his shoulder harder into the door. Desirée strained to figure out which direction the shout came from, when suddenly where there had only been a single voice before, there were many, and they were getting louder.

"How's that door coming?" Desirée asked quietly and breathy.

"Almost got it," Diego grunted.

Desirée stood with her back to Diego, scanning the hallway, her heart pounding more loudly by the second, threatening to drown everything else out. The voices had given way to pounding footfalls.

In the blink of an eye, she felt herself pulled backwards, and found herself in darkness, a hand over her mouth.

"It's just me, don't scream," Diego whispered as he lifted his hand.

On the other side of the door, Desirée could hear the rough boots brutalizing the concrete as the men who were searching for them rushed past the door. Soon, the noise dwindled until it eventually disappeared from her senses. Feeling slightly safer than she had a moment before, she tried to gain her bearings using the faint light coming from under the door, but to no avail.

"Don't move." Diego's voice was somewhere in the dark to her right. She heard him struggling with something.

"What are you doing?" she asked.

"You'll see in a second," he responded.

"Okay." Desirée didn't mind waiting for a moment. She hadn't expected to run into an entire army in an abandoned Nazi fortification, and a second to not think or do something was welcome. There was a click from Diego's direction, and suddenly the room they were in was flooded with light. She blinked back tears from the sudden change. The room that she was in was fairly large, and shockingly unworn for how long it must have lain unused. There was a large table in the middle surrounded by several long leather couches. Along the walls sat shelves, full of long forgotten books. In one of the corners there was a desk, and there was a door in the middle of each wall. One for the hallway they had just been tossed in from, and three others whose purpose yet remained unknown. Diego was standing at an old light switch, grimacing, "It could be worse, I suppose, though I'm not quite sure how."

Desirée returned his expression. She had rushed headlong into all of this, confident that she was right and had it all figured out. 'There's no way you could have anticipated Charlotte being literally insane,' she reminded herself.

"We're lucky though. I was able to grab my backpack again." He swung it around to his front and went to put it on the table. "We have some time to figure out a plan."

Desirée looked at him perplexed, "How exactly do you propose do get us out of this situation? In case you didn't notice, there's thousands of men in this bunker! How did she manage to get an army here without anyone seeing?"

"I thought about that, and I'm still working on it. From my fight, we heard that they weren't Spanish. So they're not following her out of any patriotic love."

"Okay, so she has a bunch of mercenaries, but that doesn't answer the question."

Diego shook his head, "I don't know," he admitted. "My only guess is that there must be multiple ways into this base, not just through the valley."

"Diego, we have to get out and warn everyone

of Charlotte's plan."

"You're absolutely right. Anyway, what do you know of military installations?"

Desirée sighed, "Obviously not much. Why?"

Diego sat down and started spreading the contents of his backpack on the table. "Because," he began, "any construction that is this deep underground requires a massive ventilation network. Otherwise, carbon dioxide would build up and kill everyone."

"We're going to climb through the air ducts?" Desirée didn't like the sound of that.

"Not if we don't have to, although we may have to," Diego responded flatly, "but, my thinking is that the Germans are and have always been a redundant people. They like to build failsafes into their systems. It's quite admirable in my opinion. What's the saying, something about German engineering?"

Desirée was getting impatient, "your point?"

"My point is that we are in the Officer Quarters, and it wouldn't surprise me if there were another way out of here besides the door we just came in through."

"You really think so?"

"Only one way to find out!"

Diego was still shuffling through the spilled innards of his backpack. Desirée took a look over it. There were the flashlights they had used earlier, a pair of handcuffs, some water, emergency rations, and what looked like a radio. Something was missing, but she couldn't place it. Suddenly, she realised.

"Why don't you have a gun?" Desirée asked, "James Bond has a gun."

Diego, tilted his head and gave her a nonplussed stare, "For the record, while I do have one, I don't have it with me. I lost it on the train. Quick question though, how would you expect me to shoot my way out of this situation?"

Desirée retreated, "That's a fair point, I had just thought it might come in handy."

Diego returned to his sorting, "Oftentimes, guns can serve more as a hindrance than anything else. Agents very rarely find themselves in a day to day situation where they need a firearm. In fact, it can often make a tense situation tenser, especially since I rarely track violent criminals." He began replacing everything in the bag, and then handed one of the flashlights to Desirée. "Let's take a look, shall we?"

They entered the door to the left of the entrance. It was a small bedroom. Desirée scanned, there was a bed, a closet, a writing desk, and an electric lamp on the desk that had probably long since burnt out. Diego went to the closet and opened it, it was empty. He shined the flashlight around. He shook his head, "Nothing."

They went to the next door directly opposite of the entrance, and were greeted by the same thing. Fingers crossed, they went to the final door. They opened it and Diego flipped the lights on. It was a much larger room than the prior two. "This must have been for the commanding officer," Diego commented. That made sense to Desirée. Where the other rooms had been comfy, if small, this room was easily 100 square feet. What made Desirée excited though, was that it had a couple of doors itself. Desirée went to the nearest and opened up what must have been the commander's office. On the far wall was a fireplace, and in front of it was a large oaken desk. The walls were lined with bookcases, and they were stuffed. Diego nearly jumped for joy, "Desirée, this is exactly what I was looking for!"

"It is?"

"Yes! Don't you see? There's a fireplace here! This must be the secret passageway I hoped for!"

Desirée looked at the fireplace. It didn't seem particularly notable to her, in fact, it looked like it was only decorative.

"Hang tight, I'll have us out in no time!"

Desirée shook her head, maybe he was right. She decided to take a look at the books. She pulled one off the shelves it read, *Platon Der Staat.* She put it back. She ran her finger along the edge of the shelf, looking at the spines writ over in German, now and then taking another book out before replacing it. She could hear Diego cursing in the background as he kept examining the fireplace. Out of the corner of her eye above her she saw the spine of a book that looked English. She craned her neck and read: *Through the Looking-Glass* by Lewis Carrol. She smiled, she had always loved *Alice in Wonderland,* even though the hookah smoking caterpillar had scared her as a child. She reached up and grabbed it, but it was stuck. She pulled a little harder, and... *CLICK* the entire bookcase shuddered. Diego turned, "What did you do?"

Desirée smiled, "I think I found our way out." She gave a light push on the bookcase and it gave way into a staircase that ascended into shadow. Diego walked over and shined his flashlight up the stairs. They went further than the light could follow.

Diego looked up into the darkness, "Want to see where this goes?"

Desirée nodded, wherever it went, it offered them more hope than where they were currently standing. Diego moved forward and motioned for her to follow. They began to ascend the stone steps when the light behind them disappeared suddenly. They spun around just as the bookcase slammed shut, sealing them in. Desirée ran to where the opening had just been. She couldn't see any particular mechanism to open it from her side. She slumped against the wall. She was afraid they were trapped, and from the look on Diego's face, the same fear had crossed his mind. 'Focus,' she ordered herself. They were in this predicament, and it was fine to be scared, but she was old and experienced enough to know that falling apart now wouldn't solve anything. She looked to Diego, his face had become impassive.

"Only one thing to do." He turned, and started up the stairs. Desirée got up and followed.

She swung her flashlight around from side to side, looking for anything out of place, but all she could see were the stone cut stairs, and the blank, stone walls carved from the mountain's heart. She could see Diego a few steps ahead of her, marching tirelessly towards whatever awaited them at the top of the stairs.

"Are you alright?" she asked. She was concerned. She knew how important completing this mission had been for him, but everything had changed so rapidly.

"No, I'm not," he admitted. "We're out of our depth- I'm out of my depth. This whole situation is far worse than anyone could have predicted." He stopped and sat on one of the stone steps, "We've literally been captured by someone who not only wants the Spanish Crown, but thinks that she can take it by force, as if we still live in the Middle Ages." He shook his head, "The worst part is, she has enough men here to cause problems. She couldn't win a war, but..." His voice trailed off.

"We can still try to stop her," Desirée tried to say encouragingly. She wasn't sure if it worked, but she had to attempt something. "If we can get out of here, you have a radio in your backpack. We can call Jacques for help."

Diego looked at Desirée somberly, "You're right." He got up and started walking again. Desirée wasn't sure if he actually agreed. After another fifteen minutes of nearly silent climbing, the stairs stopped at another door. It was unmarked, and made of solid steel. Unlike most of the doors they had come upon, this one seemed in good repair. Diego put his hand on the handle, and turned it gently. It responded easily.

"Ready?" he asked. Desirée nodded and Diego opened the door.

They were both nearly knocked backwards by searing daylight and vicious cold winds. Desirée gasped in astonishment, as she walked past Diego. Passing through the lit door frame she took slow steps out onto the summit of a mountain. Desirée's hair whipped around as she tried to gain her bearings. Behind her Diego was angrily muttering under his breath in Spanish.

"We'll we're out," Desirée remarked.

"Si, but out *where?*" Diego queried.

"I'm not sure," she responded, her eyes still adjusting to the day, "but, we should be able to see the valley around here somewhere."

"Dios mios, you're right. Look."

Desirée felt Diego's hand on her head, turning it ever so gently to her left. Desirée was taken aback. She struggled to comprehend what she was seeing. It seemed like a dark cloud was hovering over the valley, as if a storm had developed solely over the town. Her heart sank as she saw what had created it. The town below had been burnt to the ground, and all that remained was charred ash and beams. Charlotte of Trastámara had announced herself to the world.

Printed in Great Britain
by Amazon